For my beautiful sons
and our most amazing journey.
—G. Peter

For C & K
—G. Parsons

Ω

Published by
PEACHTREE PUBLISHING COMPANY INC.
1700 Chattahoochee Avenue
Atlanta, Georgia 30318-2112
www.peachtree-online.com

Text © 2021 by Gareth Peter
Illustrations © 2021 by Garry Parsons

First published in Great Britain as *My Daddies* in 2021 by Puffin Books, an
imprint of the Penguin Random House group of companies whose addresses
can be found at *global.penguinrandomhouse.com*

First United States version published in 2021 by Peachtree Publishing Company Inc.

The illustrations were rendered in acrylic and pencil.
Printed in October 2020 in China
10 9 8 7 6 5 4 3 2 1
First Edition
ISBN: 978-1-68263-281-9

Cataloging-in-Publication Data is available from the Library of Congress

Adventures with My Daddies

written by **Gareth Peter**   illustrated by **Garry Parsons**

PEACHTREE
ATLANTA

My daddies are amazing.
They're funny, kind, and smart.

And when they
read me stories . . .

exciting journeys start.

Sometimes we battle **dragons**,

and find **treasure**
in their cave.

Then hunt for deadly dinosaurs

on days we're feeling brave!

Sometimes we build a rocket

and **blast off** to the moon.

Or sail to secret islands,

and fly home in a balloon.

But my daddies' **favorite** story is . . .

the one that brought them me!

Some children have two mommies,

and some, a mom and dad.

But I have **SUPER** daddies!

Who chose *me* . . .

I'm **SO** glad.

They're not the best at everything . . .

but I don't *really* care.

They both make brilliant bubble beards,

and I know
they're always there.

When I feel sad, they make me smile

and hug me every day.

And if a story scares me . . .

they chase my fears away!

My daddies are amazing—
the world's best **king and king**.

And story time with them will ALWAYS be my favorite thing!

Goodnight, Daddies.